My Mum

Anthony Browne

DOUBLEDAY

London New York Toronto Sydney Auckland

She's nice, my mum.

My mum's a fantastic cook,

and a brilliant juggler.

She's a great painter,

and the STRONGEST
woman in the world!

She's really nice, my mum.

My mum's a magic gardener.
She can make ANYTHING grow.

And she's a good fairy.
When I'm sad she can make me happy.

She can sing like an angel,

and roar like a lion.

She's really, REALLY nice, my mum.

My mum's as beautiful as a butterfly,

and as comfy
as an
armchair.

She's as soft as a kitten,

and as tough as a rhino.

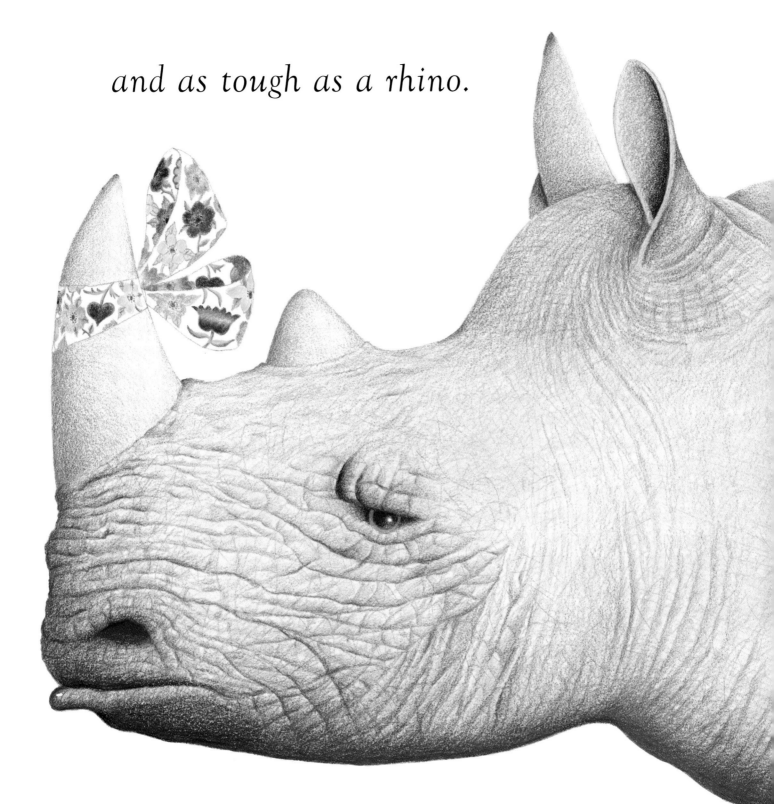

She's really, REALLY,
REALLY nice, my mum.

My mum could be a dancer,

or an astronaut.

She could be a film star,

THE BOSS

or the big boss. But she's MY mum.

She's a SUPERMUM!

And she makes me laugh. A lot.

I love my mum.

And you know what?

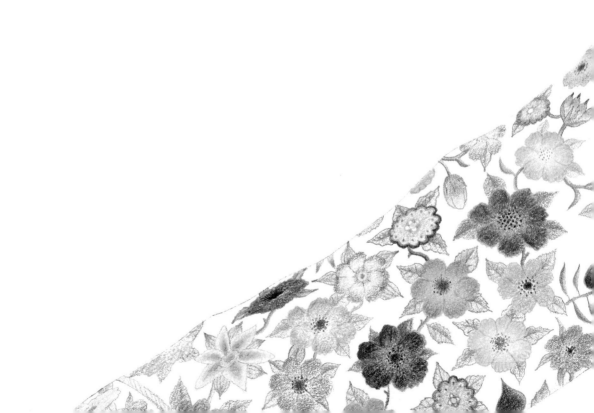

SHE LOVES ME!

(And she always will.)